Can I Come Too?

For Billy Kiddle - B.P.

For Bun and Bees - N.B.

This paperback edition first published in 2014 by Andersen Press Ltd.
First published in Great Britain in 2013 by Andersen Press Ltd.,
20 Vauxhall Bridge Road, London SW1V 2SA.
Published in Australia by Random House Australia Pty.,
Level 3, 100 Pacific Highway, North Sydney, NSW 2060.
Text copyright © Brian Patten, 2013.
Illustration copyright © Nicola Bayley, 2013.
Colour separated in Switzerland by Photolitho AG, Zürich.
Printed and bound in Malaysia by Tien Wah Press.

10   9   8   7   6   5   4   3   2   1

British Library Cataloguing in Publication Data available.

ISBN 978 1 84939 759 9

Can I Come Too?

Brian Patten & Nicola Bayley

ANDERSEN PRESS

A very small mouse decided it wanted
to have a very big adventure.
"I'll go and find the biggest creature
in the world," it thought.

By the lake it met the frog. "Are you the biggest creature in the world?" it asked.

"No," said the frog. "But it is very brave
of you to look for it. Can I come too?"
"Of course," said the mouse. "Just because
we are small doesn't mean we can't
have a big adventure."

On a branch overhanging the river they met a bird
made out of rainbows. It was the kingfisher.
"I'm a rather small bird," said the kingfisher, "but I'd
love to see what the biggest creature in the world is.
Can I come too?"

Dozing on a wall in the sunlight was the cat.
It opened an eye as they passed and said, "I'm
curious to see the biggest creature in the world.
I'll come too."

They met an otter on the riverbank
where wild flowers grew.
"Perhaps you are the biggest creature
in the world," said the mouse.

"I'm afraid not," said the otter,
"but I wonder what is?
Can I come too?"

In the wood, where everything glowed
with a green light, sat the badger.

"Its legs are far too short for it to be the biggest creature," sniffed the cat. "But I'd love to see what is," said the badger. "Can I come too?"

They crossed a little bridge in a small valley full
of tiny things. Dragonflies darted about, lizards lazed
on stones, and a water-vole washed its whiskers at the
river's edge. But they saw nothing big.
So on they went.

When they saw the dog, the cat said, "He's the scruffiest creature in the world, but he's certainly not the biggest." And the dog said, "I wonder what on earth the biggest thing is?
Can I come too?"

Halfway up a tree on the
mountainside they met the
goat. "I can see some very
large creatures from up here," it said. 
"Well, I'm looking for the biggest of them all,"
said the mouse.
And the goat said, "Can I come too?"

In the zoo they saw a tiger with paws
as big as frying pans.
"You're the most fantastic creature in
the world!" declared the mouse.
"But I'm not the biggest," said the
tiger. "If I promise not to eat anyone,
can I come too?"

The polar bear followed them out of the zoo. Its coat was as white as snow. "I know where the biggest creature in the world lives," it said. "It swims in the ocean where the river ends, and I'm going to see it now."
And the little mouse said, "Can we all come too?"

So off they went.

The mouse, the frog, the kingfisher, the otter,
the cat, the badger, the dog, the goat, the tiger
and the polar bear followed the river to the ocean.
The mouse was very excited. "I wonder what
I'm going to see?" it thought.

It was something as big as an island. Something bigger than a million mice. Seagulls flew above it. Dolphins leapt around it.

It
was the
WHALE!

The animals stood watching the whale until it plunged back beneath the waves. "We would never have seen such a wonderful thing without you," they said to the little mouse.

And the little mouse said, "I'm so glad you could all come too." Then night fell, and all the sleepy creatures decided it was time to go back home.

The mouse was so happy to have seen
the biggest creature in the world.
That night it thought to itself, "I might
be tiny, but I've had a very big adventure."
And then it curled up into a little ball
and fell fast asleep.